DISNEP

CLUB PENGUIN™

PICK YOUR PATH 3

Star Reporter

Grosset & Dunlap

Star Reporter

by Tracey West

GROSSET & DUNLAP
Published by the Penguin Group
Penguin Group (USA) Inc., 375 Hudson Street, New York,
New York 10014, USA
Penguin Group (Canada), 90 Eglinton Avenue East, Suite 700,
Toronto, Ontario M4P 2Y3, Canada
(a division of Pearson Penguin Canada Inc.)
Penguin Books Ltd., 80 Strand, London WC2R 0RL, England
Penguin Group Ireland, 25 St. Stephen's Green, Dublin 2, Ireland
(a division of Penguin Books Ltd.)
Penguin Group (Australia), 250 Camberwell Road, Camberwell,
Victoria 3124, Australia
(a division of Pearson Australia Group Pty. Ltd.)
Penguin Books India Pvt. Ltd., 11 Community Centre, Panchsheel Park,
New Delhi—110 017, India
Penguin Group (NZ), 67 Apollo Drive, Rosedale,
North Shore 0632, New Zealand
(a division of Pearson New Zealand Ltd.)
Penguin Books (South Africa) (Pty.) Ltd., 24 Sturdee Avenue,
Rosebank, Johannesburg 2196, South Africa

Penguin Books Ltd., Registered Offices:
80 Strand, London WC2R 0RL, England

© 2009 Disney. All rights reserved. Used under license by
Penguin Young Readers Group. Published by Grosset & Dunlap, a division of
Penguin Young Readers Group, 345 Hudson Street, New York, New York 10014.
GROSSET & DUNLAP is a trademark of Penguin Group (USA) Inc.
Printed in the U.S.A.

Library of Congress Control Number: 2009007019

ISBN 978-0-448-45207-4   10 9 8 7 6 5 4 3 2 1

4

A chilly wind is blowing through Club Penguin. As you leave your igloo, you're glad you wore your favorite green turtleneck and your furry boots. Your feet crunch on snow as you walk up to the door at the office of *The Club Penguin Times.*

It's nice and warm inside. The newspaper office is crowded but comfortable. Four desks form a square in the center of the room. Each desk is topped with a computer. The walls are lined with file cabinets containing back issues of *The Club Penguin Times.*

The office is bustling with activity. Penguins are running around waving papers, quickly typing at computers, and sharing ideas.

Two reporters are standing next to the water cooler in the corner. One is a yellow penguin wearing glasses and a pink hoodie. Her brown hair is tied in a side ponytail. The other is a spiffy looking brown penguin wearing a green striped polo shirt and khaki pants. A vinyl messenger bag is slung across his shoulders.

"Hi, Liz. Hi, Kip," you say. The two reporters give you a friendly wave hello and go back to their conversation.

You waddle over to one of the desks and sit down. You've only just started reporting for the newspaper, and you're a little nervous every time you come to the office. Liz and Kip are real pros. They've both had stories printed on the paper's front page.

The front page . . . You sigh just thinking about it. Imagine how cool it would be to see your story highlighted on the front page of the paper! You picture walking through the Coffee Shop, where every penguin is reading the newspaper.

"This is the best story ever!" a penguin might say.

"I must admit . . . I wrote it," you reply modestly.

"You wrote it?" the other penguin will ask in disbelief. "It's amazing!"

Kip interrupts your daydream.

"So are you ready for the staff meeting?" he asks.

"Staff meeting? What staff meeting?" you ask.

"Aunt Arctic wants to hear our best story pitches," Kip says. "I've got some good ideas.

Front page stuff for sure. You got anything?"

"Uh . . . well . . . I . . . uh," you stammer. You're totally not prepared for this! You've got to think of something, fast.

"Good afternoon, reporters!"

You'd recognize that cheerful voice anywhere. It's Aunt Arctic, the editor-in-chief of *The Club Penguin Times*. She's green and wears cat's-eye shaped glasses. A pink hat sits on top of her head, and a yellow pencil is tucked under the brim.

"Is everyone ready for the staff meeting?" she asks.

"You bet," says Liz.

"Yep," says Kip.

"Uh . . . um . . . sure," you say nervously.

You follow Liz, Kip, and the other reporters into Aunt Arctic's office. It's very tidy. Papers are stacked neatly on top of her desk. There's a colorful round rug on the floor. In the center of the room is a round table surrounded with chairs. You take a seat.

"Now then," Aunt Arctic says. "Our next issue goes to press in six hours. I am sure you all have some wonderful story ideas to suggest."

"Sure do," Liz says. "Check this out: I'm doing an article on which games can help you earn fast coins."

"Excellent," Aunt Arctic says.

You start to sweat. That's a great idea! You search your brain for something, anything. But you've got no ideas.

"I've got one," Kip says. "I'm doing a story on the best places to play hide-and-seek with your friends."

Aunt Arctic nods. "Wonderful!"

She turns to you. "And how about you?" she asks.

Come on, come on, think! you tell yourself. But it's no use.

You sigh. "I can't think of anything," you say.

"Now, that's nothing to worry about," Aunt Arctic assures you. "Every good reporter needs inspiration once in awhile."

You start to feel better. Aunt Arctic just said you were a good reporter!

"So how do I get inspiration?" you ask.

"I always find it useful to listen to what other penguins are talking about," Aunt Arctic advises. "Head into the Town Center eyes and ears open. I'm sure you'll ge in no time."

You jump up. "I'll do it! Thanks, Au

"You're welcome," she says. "But d The deadline for your story is just hours away."

You go back out into the cold and waddle to the Town Center as quickly as you can.

The Town Center is crowded with penguins. They're wandering around, talking, dancing, and waving. Aunt Arctic was right. This is a great place to learn about what's going on.

A red penguin with a blue Mohawk and a black T-shirt with a guitar on it is waddling through the crowd.

"Party at the Iceberg! Party at the Iceberg!" he shouts.

You jot this down in your reporter's notebook. A party at the Iceberg might make an interesting story.

A purple penguin in a trenchcoat and hat brushes past you. He's carrying a magnifying glass.

"Excuse me," you say. "That's an interesting outfit you're wearing."

'It's a costume," he explains. "I'm starring n *Ruby and the Ruby* down at The Stage. You should come see it!"

He hurries away as you jot down this information in your notebook. A review of the play would be a great addition to the paper.

You're still writing when a large group of noisy penguins enters the Town Center. The crowd is made up of blue penguins wearing blue jerseys, and red penguins wearing red jerseys. They're all carrying hockey sticks.

"The Blue Team is the best!" yells one of the blue penguins.

"No, the Red Team rules!" yells one of the red penguins.

"Let's get to the Ice Rink!" the blue penguin says. "We will settle this once and for all!"

There are always lots of hockey games at the Ice Rink, but this one could be special. You can just see the headline now: "Blue Team and Red Team in Super Showdown!" You quickly scribble that down on your pad.

You've only been in the Town Center for a few minutes, and you already have three story ideas. You waddle to the bench outside the Coffee Shop and sit down.

Which story should you investigate? They're all good stories. If you choose the right story, you might become the star reporter you've always wanted to be.

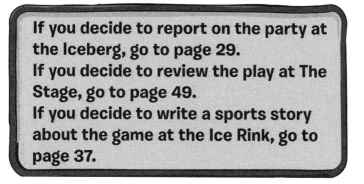

If you decide to report on the party at the Iceberg, go to page 29.
If you decide to review the play at The Stage, go to page 49.
If you decide to write a sports story about the game at the Ice Rink, go to page 37.

CONTINUED FROM PAGE 51.

You figure that the director will know what's going on. She's in charge of the play, after all. You wait until she's done talking to the crew before you approach her.

"Can I interview you for an article in *The Club Penguin Times*?" you ask.

"Sure," she replies. "But please make it quick. I've got to get ready for the next performance."

"So is the broken light fixed?" you ask.

"It should be," she replies. "Our special effects director is working on it backstage right now."

You write this down in your notebook. "Do you know why the light crashed?"

The director nods. "It's weird. It looks like somebody cut the wire it was hanging from. But that doesn't make any sense."

You look up at the ceiling, where the other lights are hanging. "That's a long way up," you say.

"Actually, Deb, our special effects director, pulled down the light earlier to change the bulb," the director says. "Maybe something happened to it then."

This is interesting. Maybe this Deb knows what happened to the light. You'll have to interview her.

"Was anyone else around while Deb was changing the bulb?" you ask her.

The director thinks for a moment. "Sure. Roy was hanging around. He's one of the extras. He likes to get here early before the show."

You write down Roy's name in your notebook and close it shut. "Thanks for your time," you say. "Good luck with the next show."

"Thanks," the director replies. "We could use it. Ever since this play started, things have been going wrong."

Intrigued, you open your notebook again. "What kinds of things?"

Before the director can answer, Kip walks in.

"Oh, hey," he says, nodding to you. "Word on the street is that there was a big crash in here. I came to write a story about it."

"I'm already writing a story about it," you say.

Kip nods. "Sure, sure," he says. "I don't mean to step on your flippers. Tell you what. I'll hang around here in case you need some help, okay?

"Okay," you reply. But you really want to prove you can write the story yourself. How else will you become a star reporter?

You walk to a corner and look over your notes. This story is starting to sound like a real-life mystery. Why are things going wrong with the play? There are two penguins who might know what happened to the light: Deb and Roy. You should talk to them before Kip gets to them. But who should you talk to first?

If you talk to Roy, the extra, go to page 33.
If you talk to Deb, the special effects director, go to page 59.

CONTINUED FROM PAGE 80.

"How about a snowball throwing competition?" you suggest. "The penguin who hits the target on the Club Penguin clock the most times out of ten wins."

The Blue Team captain grins. "Let's do this!"

The members of the Blue Team and the Red Team follow you to the Snow Forts, where the clock is located.

When you get there, the Red Team captain flips a coin to see who will throw first. You call tails. But the coin lands, and it's heads.

"Blue Team captain aims first. Players will take turns until each one has thrown ten times."

The Blue Team captain aims at the target on the Club Penguin clock. She throws . . . and hits the target dead center! The wheels of the clock spin around. The Blue Team cheers.

It's your turn next. You pack a snowball, aim . . . and throw. But your snowball misses.

Your next throws are better—you hit the target every time. The Blue Team Captain misses her fifth throw. Now you're even.

Finally, you're both on your tenth and final

throw. You've each got eight hits. The Blue Team captain tries for her ninth, and misses. You've still got one shot left. If you make it, you'll win.

The Red Team is cheering so loud you can barely concentrate. You aim and throw.

Bam! You hit the target. You did it! You won!

The Blue Team captain is not ready to give up. "Best of three?" she asks.

You are swept away by the thrill of competition. "Sure. But let's do something else."

Penguins in the crowd shout out ideas.

"*Mancala*!" says one.

"*Sled Racing*!" says another.

"Extreme Jetpack Surf Carts!" yells a third penguin, jumping up and down excitedly.

You're pretty sure that Extreme Jetpack Surf Carts isn't real, but you like the first two suggestions . . . Which one will it be?

**If you play *mancala*, go to page 26.
If you compete in *Sled Racing*,
go to page 71.**

CONTINUED FROM PAGE 72.

You decide to set the Pizzatron 3000 to make regular pizzas. Then you go into the kitchen and face the pizza-making machine. You've made hundreds of pizzas with it, and you know exactly what to do: an order will pop up on the screen. When the pizza crusts zoom by on the conveyor belt, you'll add sauce and toppings to complete the order.

The Red Team captain sets the rules. "The player to make the most pizzas without making a mistake wins." This sounds good to everyone.

The Blue Team captain goes first. She's really fast. She makes twenty-five pizzas and then she gets an order for a pizza with hot sauce, cheese, two pieces of seaweed, and two pieces of shrimp. She tries to add the last shrimp but it slides off the pizza onto the conveyor belt. Her turn is over—it's your turn now.

Focus! you tell yourself as you face the machine. You've got to win this, or there won't be a rematch. You take a deep breath as the conveyor belt starts to roll.

The first few pizzas are easy—just sauce and

cheese. Then the conveyor belt speeds up, and the orders get more complicated. But you're in the zone. Five shrimp? No problem. Squid and seaweed? *Bam! Bam!* Your flippers fly as you make pizza after pizza.

Before you know it, the buzzer rings. You've made forty pizzas without making a mistake! It's your personal record.

"I won!" you shout.

The Blue Team captain pats you on the back. "Guess we'll have that rematch now. Want to be on my team?"

You are truly surprised. "Really?"

"I like your competitive spirit," she says. "We could use a player like you."

"Of course!" you say. "I just need to buy a blue jersey at the Sport Shop. I'll meet you at the rink in five."

You grab your hockey stick, buy the blue jersey, and head to the rink. Now you're not just reporting on the game—you're playing in it! It's a close game, but this time, the Blue Team wins fair and square.

The Red Team captain congratulates you.

"Great game," he says. "Thanks for making

the rematch happen. I don't mind losing this way."

You feel great. Playing on a team is so much fun! You rush back to the office and write a whole new story.

Do you sit in the stands, wishing you could join in when you see penguins playing a game? Don't be shy! Join the team. Win or lose, you'll have a great experience.

You're happy with your story, and so is Aunt Arctic. She publishes it in the next day's issue of *The Club Penguin Times* on page B1. It's not the main story of the issue, but she highlights it with a small box on the front page!

THE END

CONTINUED FROM PAGE 39.

You don't think you can convince the Blue Team captain to have a rematch. You slink away and go back to the newspaper office, where you type up your story. You even include the fact that your camera flash blinded the Red Team's goalie as the Blue Team made the winning goal.

Aunt Arctic likes your story, especially your honesty. She puts the it in section B.

The next day, you head to the Coffee Shop. Every penguin is reading the paper. You spot Kip and Liz reading a copy on one of the couches.

"Hey," Liz calls out in a friendly tone. "Sounds like you had bad timing yesterday."

You shrug. "I just wanted to snap a great photo."

"Maybe we should call you Snap Happy," Kip says jokingly.

Liz grins. "Snap Happy. Not a bad nickname," she says.

Oh well, you think. You always wanted a reporter nickname. Now you have one!

THE END

CONTINUED FROM PAGE 68.

It's tempting to meet the mystery caller. But Aunt Arctic is the editor-in-chief of the paper, and you want to make her happy. You head to the Pizza Parlor.

The popular hangout is crowded, as usual. There are no empty seats at the small, round tables. A musician is seated at the piano, playing a mellow tune. But the atmosphere is anything but mellow. Busy waiters snake through the crowd, carrying trays of steaming pizzas.

You decide to start by interviewing the Pizza Parlor manager, who is standing behind the register. The black penguin looks spiffy in a black jacket, white shirt, and bowtie.

"I'm doing a story for the newspaper on popular pizza topping combinations," you say. "Can you tell me about your top-selling pizzas?"

"Well, the most popular pizza is our basic cheese pizza," the manager begins. "But if you want to know about combinations, there are a few that are hot right now—and I mean hot! Spicy Seaweed is always a big seller. So is the Hot Fish Dish—that's a pizza with hot sauce,

cheese, squid, and anchovies."

Just hearing about the pizzas makes your mouth water. "Thanks," you say.

You decide to interview some penguins to find out what they like. You go from table to table, talking to customers. A bunch of penguins wearing bee costumes tell you they like Seaweed Shrimp pizza best. A rock band orders an extra-hot pizza with everything on it and gets you to try some. They even invite you to their concert.

You go back to the newspaper office and start your story.

Are you in a pizza rut? Do you order the same cheese pizza every day? Try some of these sizzling combinations to spice up your diet . . .

Aunt Arctic returns from feeding her puffles. You show her your story and she loves it.

"How would you like to be our official Food and Entertainment reporter?" she asks.

"I would love that!" you say.

You feel really proud. You're a brand-new reporter and you already have your own beat!

THE END

CONTINUED FROM PAGE 70.

You decide to check out the Pet Shop first. A bell chimes as you step through the doors. Large shelves hold boxes of Puffle-Os and pet treats. Puffle beds, bowls, and houses are scattered across the floor.

Six puffles bounce happily in a pen in the middle of the room. A frowning black puffle stares at you from a birdcage on a stand. A red puffle freely wanders the shop. It passes a yellow puffle who looks comfortable on top of a sack of puffle food.

You take a minute to say hi to the puffles in the pen. They're so cute! But you don't have time to play. You've got a story to write.

You go to the cash register and lift it up. There's nothing underneath. You feel around with your flipper, but there's no clue. You sigh. Looks like you went to the wrong place.

"Excuse me, I'd like to buy this puffle scratching post." A pink penguin is at the counter, holding up her purchase.

"Oh, I don't work here," you say. You quickly back away from the register. You've got to get to the Pizza Parlor.

Then you feel something brush against your boots. You look down and see a yellow puffle with purple and red spots bouncing next to you!

You can't believe your luck. Puffles come in all kinds of colors, but you've never seen a spotted puffle before. This is big news! The Iceberg photo can wait for now. You want to write the story that's right here in front of you.

You want to rush to get the story to Aunt Arctic. But then you stop—maybe you should investigate a little more to see where the spotted puffle came from.

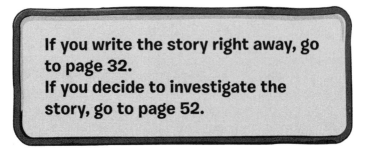

If you write the story right away, go to page 32.
If you decide to investigate the story, go to page 52.

CONTINUED FROM PAGE 62.

You don't want Kip to scoop you. You hurry
back to the newspaper office and write your
story. Then you give it to Aunt Arctic.

She sits at her desk and reads it. "This is a
very interesting story," she says. "However, you
need more information. Nobody actually saw Deb
cause the accidents. It's not right to print the
story without all of the facts. It's unfair to Deb."

Aunt Arctic sees how upset you look. "Don't
be discouraged! It's a very good effort for a first-
time reporter. Why don't you try writing a story
for next week's issue?"

You know Aunt Arctic is right. "Thanks,"
you say. "I'll do better next time."

Just as you feared, Kip scoops you with a
story about the play. He discovers that Deb's
puffle was causing all the accidents. Turns out
Deb forgot to feed it, so it was eating the props!
You head back to the Town Center to find some
new leads. This time, you will get all the facts
before you write.

THE END

CONTINUED FROM PAGE 16.

"How about one game of *mancala*?" you suggest. "Winner of the game wins the round."

"It's a deal," says the Blue Team captain. The gleam in her eye makes you nervous. She looks extremely confident.

You head to the Book Room with the crowd of penguins. You and the Blue Team captain sit down at a *mancala* board. She goes first and immediately scores an extra turn. You quickly find out why she looked so confident. She's a *mancala* whiz, capturing your stones every time she takes a turn. The game ends when her side of the board is empty. She's got way more stones in her *mancala* than you.

"I win!" she says. "We've got one more round. What will it be? A swim race in the Underground Pool, or the *Dance Contest* in the Night Club?"

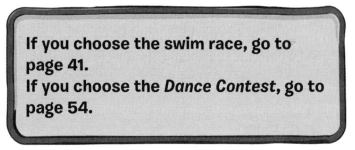

If you choose the swim race, go to page 41.
If you choose the *Dance Contest*, go to page 54.

CONTINUED FROM PAGE 64.

You will feel very silly if you go to the Mine Shack just to get pummeled by snowballs again. You decide to stop following the story.

You quickly head to the Pizza Parlor. You talk to the manager and customers there, scribbling down notes on your pad. When you think you've got enough for your story, you rush down to the newspaper office.

As you walk in, you see Aunt Arctic standing over Kip's desk. She's reading a story printout.

"This is an excellent report on popular pizza topping combinations," she says. "But I did assign the story to someone else."

"Yes," you say. "Me!"

Kip nods. "I overheard Aunt Arctic assign the story to you. I went to the Pizza Parlor to see if I could help. When I didn't see you there, I figured I should do some research just in case. But if you already wrote something . . ."

"No, I didn't write my story yet," you admit. "I was following another lead. But it didn't work out."

You turn to Aunt Arctic. "Go ahead and use Kip's story," you say sadly. "I'll work on another story for next week."

Aunt Arctic gives you a kind smile. "I know you'll come up with something great!"

THE END

CONTINUED FROM PAGE 11.

You have been to Iceberg parties before. They're always fun, and sometimes interesting things happen. If it's a really great party, you can write a colorful review. So you decide to head to the Iceberg.

When you arrive, the Iceberg is crowded with penguins. You start to feel excited. There's got to be a story here somewhere.

Most of the penguins are standing on a ridge on the back of the Iceberg. They're wearing orange construction helmets and drilling into the ice with jackhammers.

"Tip the Iceberg!" somebody shouts.

"Drill! Drill!"

"Come on! Let's tip it!"

You have seen this happen before. Many penguins believe that if enough penguins drill into the Iceberg, it will tip into the ocean. You have been to tipping parties yourself. You drilled and drilled, but nothing happened.

You decide to hang around and see if the Iceberg tips—that would be a huge story. In the meantime, you interview some penguins.

You tap an orange penguin on the shoulder. "Excuse me," you say. "I'm a reporter for *The Club Penguin Times*. Mind if I ask you some questions?"

"Sure!" the penguin shouts over the sound of the jackhammer.

"So, have you ever seen the Iceberg tip before?" you ask.

"No," the penguin replies. "But a friend of a friend of mine said he saw it tip."

You write this down, excited. "Really? What was his name?"

The penguin shrugs. "I can't remember. But I'm sure it's true."

"Thanks," you say. You walk away, frowning. You can't print what the penguin just told you—it's a rumor. What you need is some real proof. Aunt Arctic herself has said that she has never seen proof that the Iceberg tipped.

You start to think that coming to the Iceberg was a bad idea. You walk away from the drilling penguins and stand at the edge of the Iceberg, gazing at the sea. You're not sure what to do.

Then you hear a sound behind you.

"Psssst."

You turn around and see a black penguin with a baseball cap pulled low over his face.

"You looking for proof that the Iceberg tipped?" he asks.

"I sure am," you reply. "Do you know where I can find it?"

The penguin nods. "I do."

"Great!" you reply. "I have a few questions for you. First, what's your name?"

"That's not important," the penguin says mysteriously. "I can tell you where to find the proof you need. But it will be a difficult search."

The penguin is sure acting strange. Is he serious? You look at your watch. Time is passing quickly. You really want to get a story into the next issue. There's still time to write a review of the party. Or, you could listen to the mysterious penguin's story about the Iceberg. But will you end up on a wild goose chase?

If you decide to write a review of the Iceberg party, go to page 40. If you talk to the mysterious penguin, go to page 69.

CONTINUED FROM PAGE 24.

You rush back to the office and write up your story. Then you show it to Aunt Arctic.

"A spotted puffle! How wonderful," Aunt Arctic says. "We need more information before we can put a story like this on the front page, but I'll put it in the first section. We can call it, 'The Mystery of the Spotted Puffle.'"

You're very excited when the story comes out the next day. You go to the newspaper office, ready to work on the follow-up to your story. Aunt Arctic and Liz are waiting for you.

"Liz has exciting news." Aunt Arctic says. "She solved the mystery of the spotted puffle!"

You're confused. "She has?"

Liz nods. "Yup. I went down to the Pet Shop yesterday. Turns out the spotted puffle is really a yellow puffle that got into some paint. I saw the paint on the floor. Then I gave the puffle a bath."

"Oh, that's great," you say. But you don't feel great. Liz scooped your story! You wish you had taken the time to investigate the story yourself.

THE END

CONTINUED FROM PAGE 14.

You decide to talk to Roy. You find the extras' dressing room backstage. There are four blue penguins inside.

"Can I please talk to Roy?" you ask. "I'm from *The Club Penguin Times*."

One of the penguins looks up. "That's me!" he says, waddling over to you. "Are you going to interview me about my role in the play?" He sounds very excited.

"Actually, I wanted to ask you about the light that crashed," you say. "The director says you were here early, when the light bulb was being changed. Did you see anything happen to the wire on the light?"

Roy frowns. "Oh, that," he says. "I thought you were going to ask me about being an actor."

You feel bad for Roy. "Oh, I will," you say. "I just wanted to ask you about the light first."

"I didn't see a thing," he says, "Now let me tell you about myself. Can you believe I'm an extra in this play! I don't even know why we have a dressing room. We don't have any costumes."

"But extras are important," you say.

"I don't even get to speak!" Roy says. "My talent is wasted here. You want a great story? I've got one. Follow me."

You haven't finished your story about the crash yet, but Roy is an interesting guy. Curious, you follow him.

Roy takes you to the Lighthouse. A penguin is onstage, reading poetry out loud.

"We have poetry readings here all the time," Roy tells you. "Check this out."

Roy hops onstage next. He starts to read his poem in a loud, dramatic voice:

The Beacon is the place to be,
If you want to gaze out at the sea . . .

Roy's voice is a little too loud and squeaky. You can understand why he didn't get a speaking part in the play. But his poem is really good. You tell Roy he should submit his poems to *The Club Penguin Times.*

Aunt Arctic loves Roy's poems and puts one of them in the next issue. You didn't get a story into the paper, but that's okay with you. You're glad you made Roy happy.

THE END

CONTINUED FROM PAGE 80.

You're a pretty good ice hockey player. And since you're already at the rink, you might as well stay.

"Let's see who can make the most goals out of ten," you say. "I'll shoot against your goalie, and you can shoot against the Red Team goalie to keep it fair."

She nods, and her side-tied ponytail bounces up and down. "Best of ten. Let's do this. I'll go first."

The Red Team goalie takes his place. The Blue Team captain stands on the center line of the ice and takes her first shot.

Wham! The puck zips across the ice and past the goalie. Her first shot is in.

You're starting to think this wasn't a good idea. The Blue Team captain proceeds to make nine shots out of ten! You're not sure if you can beat that. But you've got to try.

You take your position and get ready for your first shot. You shoot, but the Red Team goalie stops the puck.

"I've got to stay cool if I'm going to make

35

the next shot," you say. "Hey, you know the best way for hockey players to stay cool? To stand near the fans!"

Everybody laughs at your joke, and you relax. "I'd better not make any more jokes out here. I don't want the ice to crack up. Get it? *Crack up!*"

Everyone laughs again. You take your next shot—and miss again. There's no point in shooting anymore. You can't beat the Blue Team captain's score.

You skate over to the Red Team captain. "Sorry about that," you say.

"It's okay," he says. "You tried. Besides, you're pretty funny. You should submit some of those jokes to the newspaper."

You like the Red Team captain's idea. You head back to the office and type up some jokes for Aunt Arctic. She loves them! You're happy. Who needs the front page when you can make people laugh?

THE END

CONTINUED FROM PAGE 11.

It sounds like a good game is heating up at the Ice Rink, so you head there. You climb onto the top row of the bleachers so you'll get a good view of the game. The Red Team and the Blue Team are already on the ice.

On the sidelines, cheerleaders in red yell, "Go, Red Team, go!"

Cheerleaders dressed in blue yell, "Go, Blue! We love you!"

It's a fast-paced game as the puck zips across the ice. The goalies on both teams are good, but the other players are quick. The game is evenly matched. First the Red Team scores, then the Blue Team, then the Red Team . . .

You write down every exciting pass, every goal. The score is 5-5, a tie. A referee on the ice is keeping time.

"Thirty seconds!" he yells.

You suddenly realize that while you have taken notes, you don't have any photos of the game. A photo would be a great addition to your story. You scramble down to the bottom of the bleachers and point your camera at the players.

A player from the Blue Team is advancing on the Red Team's goal. He raises his hockey stick, ready to shoot. You take a photo as the puck zips through the air toward the goalie.

Flash! Your camera flash goes off, blinding the goalie.

"Hey!" the goalie yells. The puck flies past her and slams into the net.

The referee's whistle pierces through the roar of the crowd.

"Goal, Blue Team!" the referee announces. "Blue Team wins, six to five."

The Red Team captain stomps over to the referee. "Are you kidding?" he says. "That reporter blinded my goalie! That shouldn't count."

You blush. The captain is talking about you! You feel terrible.

"The puck landed in the Red Team goal," the referee says. "I have to call it for the Blue Team."

The Blue Team captain gives the Red Team captain a friendly pat on the back. "Better luck next time!" she says.

"No way!" the Red Team captain says. "I demand a rematch!"

"But the ref says it's fair," the Blue Team captain replies.

You feel bad about your camera flash interfering with the game. "It was my fault," you say. "Maybe a rematch isn't a bad idea."

The Blue Team captain shakes her head. "I don't think so."

If you go back to the office and file your story, go to page 20.
If you stick around to convince the Blue Team captain to try a rematch, go to page 80.

CONTINUED FROM PAGE 31.

You don't trust the mysterious penguin. You decide to write a review of the party instead.

You walk through the crowd, talking to the penguins you meet. Everyone's having a great time. You even meet the red penguin with the blue Mohawk, who started the party.

"Let's be friends," he says. "I throw lots of parties. You should come to the next one."

"Thanks!" you say. "That would be great."

You head back to the newspaper office and type up your party review. Then you print it out and bring it to Aunt Arctic. You stand in front of her desk while she reads it.

"Hmm," she says. "Hmm." Then she looks up. "This is a very entertaining review. I have just the spot for it on page C3."

You're happy, but a little disappointed, too. You didn't make the front page.

You head back into the Town Center to get more ideas. Today's deadline may be over, but you can always try for next week's front page.

THE END

CONTINUED FROM PAGE 26.

The two choices are interesting, but you know you're a pretty good swimmer.

"Let's do the swim race," you say.

You leave the Coffee Shop and go to the Gift Shop first. You and the Blue Team captain use the dressing rooms to change into swimsuits. Then you walk next door to the Night Club.

You all march into the secret entrance to the Boiler Room, located in one of the speakers. You climb a ladder into the Boiler Room, and then walk through a door into the room that holds the pool.

Through the three large windows on the wall you can see fish and crabs swimming through the water. A rope strung with small buoys divides the long pool into two lanes. You and the Blue Team captain each stand at the edge of the pool, on either side of the rope.

"First penguin to the other side wins," says the Red Team captain. "I'll count you off. On your mark, get set, go!"

You dive in and swim as fast as you can. The crowd cheers both of you on. You're splashing like crazy when you reach the other side. Your flipper touches the wall of the pool—but did you win?

You lift your head out of the water, gasping for breath. Your heart sinks when you see that the Blue Team captain has already climbed out of the pool.

"Two out of three. I win," she says. She reaches down to help you out. "You're tough competition."

"Thanks," you say. You turn to the Red Team captain. "Sorry you won't get a rematch."

The Red Team captain shrugs. "You tried hard to make it happen. There's always next time."

Instead of writing about the game for the newspaper, you write a profile of both team captains. Aunt Arctic likes the story, and both captains are really flattered. You've made it into the paper—and you've made two new friends as well.

THE END

CONTINUED FROM PAGE 57.

You decide to choose the old-fashioned way.

"Eenie, meenie, miney, mo . . ." you chant. You end up pointing at Ridge Run.

"Here goes nothing," you say. You grab a red snow tube and head down the hill.

Ridge Run is a challenging course. There are lots of obstacles to jump over and patches of icy water to avoid. You do your best, but it's a bumpy ride.

When you land at the bottom of the hill, you hop off of your tube and start to dig. You shovel for a minute or two when you hear a loud *clang*. Your shovel has hit something!

Excited, you bend down and begin to dig with your hands. You pull out a small metal box. You lift the lid. Inside is an envelope with "Iceberg Tipping Photo" printed on it. You've found it!

You take the envelope out of the box and start to open it. Then you hear a scream behind you.

"Whoooaaaaaaa!"

A penguin is tumbling down the hill on

a snow tube at lightning speed. He's out of control. Before you can move out of the way . . .

Bam! He slams into you, knocking you down. The envelope flies out of your hand.

"Noooo!" you cry. You reach for the envelope, but it lands in a mound of wet snow.

The penguin on the snow tube stands up, brushing snow from his pants.

"Sorry about that," he says. "That's a tough course."

"It's okay," you say. You know the penguin didn't mean to knock you down. You just hope the photo isn't ruined.

You recover the envelope. It's wet and falling apart in your flipper. You open it up and pull out the photo. The ink has smeared all over. It looks like a photo of a blurry rainbow. If the photo really was proof that the Iceberg tipped, it's useless now.

You feel so bad about the photo that you don't write your story. You'll just have to try again next week.

THE END

CONTINUED FROM PAGE 72.

You decide to make candy pizzas. Everyone heads to the Pizza Parlor. You ask the manager if you can use the Pizzatron 3000 for a little while to hold your contest. He checks with his customers to see if they're in the mood for candy pizza, and you're in luck. The contest is on!

You step behind the curtain into the kitchen and walk up to the Pizzatron 3000.

"Each player will take a turn on the machine," says the Red Team captain. "The player to make the most correct orders without making a mistake wins."

The Blue Team captain goes first. The orders flash on a screen on the machine, and empty pizza crusts begin to whiz by on a conveyor belt. She scrambles to add the correct candy topping for each order.

She's pretty fast, and makes seventeen pizzas correctly before she makes a mistake. Then it's your turn. You've never made candy pizzas before, and after you make five pizzas you're a chocolate-covered mess. You've got to add three marshmallows to your pizzas but your hands are too sticky to grab them. You lose!

The Blue Team captain waddles up to you. "Good game," she says. "I'd shake your flipper but it's kind of sticky."

You go back to your igloo and clean up. Then you head to the newspaper office to write your story. You don't feel like writing about the ice hockey game anymore. Instead, you write an article with tips for making candy pizza.

THE END

CONTINUED FROM PAGE 70.

You decide to go check out the Pizza Parlor first. The smell of hot, delicious pizza hits you as soon as you enter. The place is crowded, as always. There are penguins sitting at tables, eating. Other penguins wearing aprons and chef's hats are serving pizza. A cashier sits at the register in front of a beaded curtain that leads the way to the kitchen.

You walk up to the cashier, a purple penguin with blond hair.

"Um, do you mind if I look under your cash register?" you ask.

She shrugs. "Sure. Whatever."

"Thanks!" you say. You lift up the end of the cash register and see a piece of paper peeking out. You've found the next clue! You quickly grab it. Then you hurry to a corner of the room so you can read it.

Go to this building and open the door.
Head up to the second floor.
Act like a moth and follow the light.
And the next clue will be in sight.

Your mind is racing. You think about the buildings in Club Penguin that have two floors. You know there's the Book Room above the Coffee Shop, and the Ski Lodge has an Attic. There must be more, but that's all you can think of now. You have to decide where to go first!

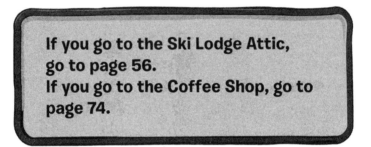

If you go to the Ski Lodge Attic, go to page 56.
If you go to the Coffee Shop, go to page 74.

CONTINUED FROM PAGE 11.

You know if you write a good review of the play, you'll probably get into the paper. It might not make the front page, but if you do a good job you will impress Aunt Arctic. You can work your way up to the front page.

You head to the Plaza. The Stage is nestled between the Pet Shop and the Pizza Parlor. The marquee over the entrance is outlined with globe-shaped lights. They shine on the title of the play: *Ruby and the Ruby*.

A penguin behind the ticket booth gives you a ticket and you step inside the darkened theater. A purple penguin in a brown director's cap is organizing the actors onstage. The play is about to begin.

You saw *Ruby and the Ruby* the last time it played in The Stage. The black-and-white set looks like something out of an old movie. The stage is divided into three sections: the office of a private eye, a deserted street corner, and the lobby of a fancy hotel.

You quietly take a seat and watch the action unfold. The action starts in the private eye's

office. A black penguin dressed in a trench coat and hat is seated behind the desk. He's Hammer, the private eye.

A red penguin wearing a blond wig, pearls, and a pink, sparkly dress rushes in.

"You've got to help me!" Ruby wails.

Hammer sits up straight. "What's the matter, madam?"

"Someone has stolen my gemstone!" she cries.

The action continues as Hammer goes to the city street to interview a suspect named Tenor. He is dressed in a blue zoot suit, porkpie hat, and skinny tie. A few blue penguins playing his henchmen are gathered behind him.

Hammer is questioning Tenor when . . .

BAM! One of the stage lights crashes down from the ceiling. The whole theater goes dark.

"Everyone stay calm!" the director yells. She rushes onto the stage.

Nobody is hurt, but the stage is a mess. The director turns to the audience. "Sorry, but we'll have to end the play early," she says. "Please come to our next show."

The lights flicker on. You're disappointed.

You want to write a review, but it will be short. Then you realize—the fact that the light crashed might be a good angle for your story. You should stick around and investigate.

You write a review of the play in your notebook while some crew members clear up the stage. Then you waddle over to the stage. The director is there, telling the crew what to do. You also see the actor who plays Hammer watching from the side of the stage.

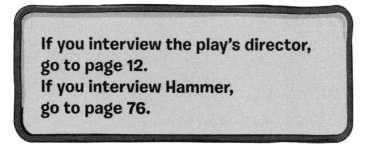

If you interview the play's director, go to page 12.
If you interview Hammer, go to page 76.

CONTINUED FROM PAGE 24.

You know you will need more information to write a good story. You lean down and talk to the puffle.

"Hey, little fella," you say. "Where did you come from?"

The spotted puffle bounces up and down. You notice what looks like a blotch of red and purple paint on the floor underneath it.

Then the puffle bounces across the floor. You follow it. As you waddle along, you notice splotches of red and purple paint everywhere. You think you may know the story behind the spotted puffle.

The puffle leads you to a secluded spot behind a sack of pet food. You see a messy paint pallette on the floor. Paint is smeared everywhere. You gently pick up the puffle.

"I think you need a bath," you say.

The spotted puffle doesn't object. You give it a nice, soapy bubble bath. The water in the tub turns bright red and purple—and you are left holding a yellow puffle.

You smile. You know that yellow puffles are

very creative and like to paint. This one must have had a little paint accident.

You're glad you solved the mystery, but you still don't have a story. Then you hear a laugh behind you.

Two pink penguins are giggling. "Aw, that puffle is so cute!" one says. "I can't believe it had all those spots on it!"

That's when you realize that the story of the spotted puffle might not be front page news, but it's still entertaining. You hurry back to the newspaper office and begin to write.

Yesterday, a spotted puffle was seen in the Pet Shop. That's right—a spotted puffle! Was this the discovery of a brand-new kind of puffle, or something else? This reporter just had to investigate . . .

You finish your story on time, and Aunt Arctic loves it. She prints it in the next issue. Liz and Kip compliment you on writing a great story. You are definitely on your way to becoming a star reporter!

THE END

CONTINUED FROM PAGE 26.

You're guessing that the Blue Team captain is a really good swimmer, so you choose the *Dance Contest*.

You all leave the Coffee Shop and head to the Night Club next door. Cadence, the DJ, is spinning a funky beat on the turntable. She's a peach penguin with pink hair, wearing green headphones and a yellow and pink striped scarf.

"Perfect," you say. Cadence judges the dancers at the *Dance Contest*. You approach her. "I need to have a dance-off with my friend here. Would you please judge us?"

"You got it!" Cadence says, smiling. "Each of you can dance for two minutes, and I'll pick the winner. Who'll go first?"

You nod to the Blue Team captain. "Be my guest," you say.

Cadence spins a new record and a groovy beat fills the air.

The Blue Team captain starts to dance. You can see why she wanted to compete in a dance contest. She's got some pretty smooth moves.

She gracefully spins off the dance floor, and

then it's your turn. You really want to win, so you use every dance move you can think of. You spin and turn and wiggle like never before.

Cadence steps out onto the floor when you're done. "Let's make some noise! That was smooth as ice!" she yells.

The crowd claps and cheers. "Rock solid moves from both of you," Cadence says. "But every contest has a winner, and I'd have to give the edge to this penguin!"

Cadence points to you. You can't believe it. You've won!

The Blue Team captain grins. "I know when I've been beat." She turns to the Red Team captain. "Time for a rematch!"

Everyone races back to the Ice Rink. The two teams play again, and this time the Red Team wins. Both teams head to the Pizza Parlor to celebrate, but you go to the newspaper office and write your story. Aunt Arctic likes you so much that she promotes you.

You're the new Head Sportswriter for *The Club Penguin Times!*

THE END

You head to the Ski Lodge. A bunch of penguins are warming up around the fire. You wave to them as you climb the ladder upstairs.

An old lamp lights up the dim Attic. *Find Four* games are propped up on old boxes and suitcases that are scattered on the floor.

You head right for the old lamp and examine it. A piece of paper is taped inside the shade. Two penguins playing *Find Four* look at you curiously as you take out the note and open it up.

> Your prize is buried under the snow.
> Grab a shovel and then you must go
> Up the Ski Hill for some fun.
> Sled down the trail that ends in 'Run'.

You're starting to feel excited. It sounds like you're close! You don't have a shovel, but you hope they have one for sale in the Sport Shop next door. Then you just have to sled down the trail that ends in "Run" . . .

You pause. There are *two* trails that end in

run—Ridge Run and Penguin Run. You'll have to test out both of them.

You race down the ladder, go outside, and head to the Sport Shop. You use up the last of your money to buy a small snow shovel.

Then you hop on the Ski Lift and ride up the mountain. You will have to sled down one of the runs to find the Iceberg tipping photo. But which run will you choose?

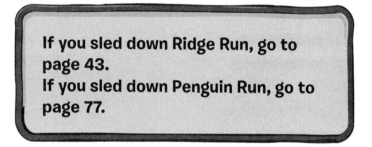

If you sled down Ridge Run, go to page 43.
If you sled down Penguin Run, go to page 77.

You go to the Mine Shack. Nobody is there. *Whack! Whack! Whack!* More snowballs hit you. You've been tricked! But then you spot another note in one of the snowballs:

WE ARE THE SURPRISE SNOWBALL SOCIETY! WE HAVE SNOWBALL FIGHTS ANY TIME, ANYWHERE. LET OTHERS KNOW WE EXIST!

Now you're glad you came. This has the makings of an interesting story. You glance at your watch. The deadline is not far off. But you can write a short story about this.

As you waddle back to the newspaper office, you see footprints in the snow. You stop. Could they belong to the mysterious note sender?

**If you try to write your story before the deadline, go to page 73.
If you follow the footprints, go to page 78.**

CONTINUED FROM PAGE 14.

Since Deb was the last penguin to touch the light, you decide to talk to her first. You find her backstage in the special effects room. The room is crowded with props and costumes from other plays. It's a real mess.

Deb is rummaging through an old trunk. She's a pink penguin with a brown Flutterby hairdo. It's held in place with a pink barrette. A red puffle sits by her feet.

"Where did I put that gallon of fog juice?" she is muttering. She doesn't see you.

"Hi, there," you say.

Deb looks up. "What? Whoa!"

Startled, she trips over a pair of silver boots on the floor. The puffle jumps out of the way. You help her up.

"Sorry, didn't mean to scare you," you say.

Deb jumps up. "That's okay. I'm a little clumsy sometimes."

The red puffle hops over to you and nudges your boot. It looks up at you with big eyes. You've seen that look in puffles before.

"You look hungry, little guy," you say.

Luckily, you have an extra cookie with you. You feed it to the puffle, who gulps it down hungrily.

"Thanks," Deb says. "I've been so busy working on this play, I barely have time to feed Fireball."

"It looks like you have a lot to do," you agree, looking around. "I hope I'm not bothering you. I'm writing an article for *The Club Penguin Times* and I was hoping to interview you."

"No problem! Just as soon as I find that fog juice," Deb says.

You spot a jug handle sticking out of the trunk. You grab it. "Is this it?" you ask.

"You found it!" Deb says happily. She rushes to bring the fog juice to her worktable. On the way, she bumps into a prop that looks like a spaceship. She drops the jug, and fog juice spills all over the floor. A mist starts to rise.

"Whoops!" Deb says. She sighs. "Guess I'll have to get more."

"I just have one question," you say. "Did you notice anything when you changed the bulb in the stage light earlier? The director says the wire was cut."

Deb shakes her head. "I don't think so. Roy

was here, reading me some of his poetry. And Fireball was here, of course. But after I changed the bulb, I hung the light right back over the stage."

You frown. You are not even close to solving this mystery.

"Oh no! My zoot suit!"

The cry is coming from the actors' dressing rooms. You nod to Deb.

"Thanks. I want to check this out."

You find the actor who plays Tenor in his dressing room. He's holding his blue zoot suit, which is all ripped up.

"What happened?" you ask.

"I don't know," Tenor says. "When the play ended early, I went to grab a slice of pizza. When I got back, my suit was ruined!"

"Did you see anyone in your dressing room?" you ask.

"Deb was in here when I left, bringing me a prop she fixed," Tenor replies.

"Hmm," you say.

Kip pokes his head in the door. "Did I hear a scream?" he asks.

"I'm interviewing Tenor," you tell him.

"Great!" Kip says cheerfully. "Let me know if you need any help. I just learned some interesting things from the director."

Kip leaves, but you are starting to feel nervous. You want to give Aunt Arctic your story fast, before Kip scoops you.

You're pretty sure that Deb is causing the accidents on the set. She's very clumsy, after all. You can see the headline now: "Mystery of Accidents at The Stage Solved!"

A little voice inside you says that you need more proof before you can write that story. Should you listen to it? If you do, you could miss your chance to get a story in the next issue of the newspaper.

If you write the article about Deb causing the accidents, go to page 25. If you decide to investigate some more, go to page 65.

CONTINUED FROM PAGE 68.

You know Aunt Arctic will understand if you try to go for the bigger story. You quickly head for the Club Penguin clock.

The clock is located in the Snow Forts, right next to the Ice Rink. Gary the Gadget Guy invented the clock so that everyone on Club Penguin would always know what time it is and could arrange to meet for parties and games. The clock is powered by snowballs, which was why Gary put it in the Snow Forts.

There are usually a few penguins in the Snow Forts, tossing snowballs at one another, or aiming them at the target on the clock. But the place is eerily deserted. You walk to the base of the clock and look up. It's been five minutes since you received the mysterious phone call. So where is the penguin who called you?

"Hello?" you call out.

There is no reply. Then . . . *whack!* A snowball hits you in the arm. Where did it come from?

Whack! Whack! Whack! More snowballs rain from the sky. You can't see who's throwing

them. Is it the mysterious caller, or is someone hiding behind a fort, having a friendly fight?

You hear giggling, and then the sound of feet crunching in the snow.

You're a little upset. Was this some kind of trick? A silly plan so some penguin could throw snowballs at you?

Then you notice something sticking out of one of the snowballs. It's a note. You pull it out of the snowball to read it: MINE SHACK, SEVEN MINUTES.

Part of you wants to crumple up the note and toss it away. It's probably just another trick.

But part of you is curious. The mysterious penguin could just be testing you, making sure you're worthy of the big story.

You're not sure what to do. If you hurry, you might have time to write the pizza story Aunt Arctic wanted.

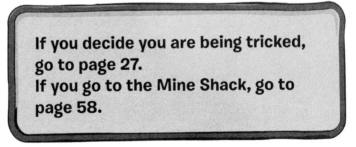

If you decide you are being tricked, go to page 27.
If you go to the Mine Shack, go to page 58.

CONTINUED FROM PAGE 62.

You haven't been a news reporter very long, but you still know that it's important to have all the facts before you write a story. You decide to stick around and investigate some more.

Tenor told you that Deb was in the room when he left to get pizza. You decide to talk to Deb again. You find her onstage, hauling the fixed light back up to the ceiling.

"Good as new," she says. "We're all ready for the next show."

"Deb, I need to ask you something else," you say. "Tenor's costume got ripped to shreds a little while ago. It happened while he went out to get pizza. Did you see anything in his dressing room when you were there before?"

Deb shakes her head. "Nope. I left the prop on his dressing table. It needed a few finishing touches, so I tinkered with it for a minute. Then Fireball and I left."

You jot down some notes in your book. Then you hear Deb yell.

"Fireball! No!"

You feel something tug at your boot.

Fireball is chewing right through the fur!

"Boy, you really are hungry, little guy," you say.

You gently pick it up. There's something in its red fur—a scrap of blue material.

Suddenly, it hits you. You know why accidents have been happening on the set!

"I figured it out!" you cry.

The director and Hammer hear you and gather around.

"I know why the light fell, and why Tenor's suit got ruined," you say. "Fireball did it. It didn't mean to—it was just hungry."

Deb slaps her flipper against her forehead. "That makes sense! I've been so busy, I keep forgetting to feed it. When it gets hungry in my igloo, it chews up all my furniture and clothes. It's probably doing the same thing here."

The director turns to you. "Thanks for solving this mystery," she says. "You can have a front row seat at The Stage any time."

"That's great!" you reply. "And now I've got to run. I've got a story to file!"

You race back to the newspaper office. You have the perfect headline in mind.

Mystery of Accidents at The Stage Solved!

Have you seen the play at The Stage? Ruby and the Ruby *is a great mystery. But there was a mystery behind the scenes, too.*

All kinds of strange accidents were happening at the play. Nobody knew why they were happening. And nobody guessed the real culprit—a hungry puffle!

You tell the whole story, including the crashed light, the ruined costume, and quotes from your interviews. Aunt Arctic waddles in as you're finishing up. She reads the article over your shoulder.

"What a fascinating story!" she says. "I think I will highlight this on the front page, above the main story."

Being highlighted above the main story is pretty good. But you still want to write the main story yourself. You're so close!

Aunt Arctic looks at the clock on the wall. "We still have a few hours before deadline, and I need one more story. You did such a good job on this one. Would you like another assignment?"

"Of course!" you say.

"I'd like to run a story on the most popular pizza topping combinations," she says.

You quickly jot this down in your notebook. "Got it," you say. "I'm off!"

"Me, too," Aunt Arctic says. "That story reminded me—I've got to go home and feed my puffles!"

Aunt Arctic leaves. You're about to go, too, when the office phone rings. You pick it up.

"I have a tip for a reporter who wants a big story," the male voice says. "If you want to know more, meet me at the Club Penguin clock in five minutes."

"Wait!" you say. "Who are you?" But the caller hangs up.

You're not sure what to do. Should you do the pizza story that Aunt Arctic wants, or go meet the mysterious caller?

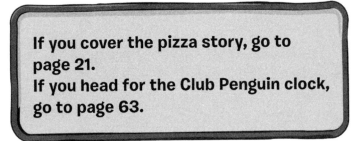

If you cover the pizza story, go to page 21.
If you head for the Club Penguin clock, go to page 63.

CONTINUED FROM PAGE 31.

You don't have much time left, but finding proof that the Iceberg tipped would put you on the front page for sure. You decide to keep talking to the mysterious penguin.

"Tell me what you know," you say.

The penguin leans over and whispers to you. His cap is pulled down so low that you can't get a good look at his face.

"There's a photo," he says.

Your eyes widen. "A photo? Really?" A photo would be just the proof you need!

"It was taken by a friend of a friend," the penguin says. "He was there when it happened. A bunch of penguins were drilling, and the Iceberg started to tip. So he swam out into the ocean and took a picture of it. It's amazing."

You scribble furiously on your pad. "So why is this penguin keeping the photo a secret?"

"He's a little bit strange," the penguin replies. "He believes only worthy penguins should see the photo."

"I really want to see it," you say. "What do I need to do?"

The penguin slips a folded piece of paper into your flipper. "Follow the clues," he says.

Then he dashes off into the crowd. You open the paper. There's a riddle written inside:

> The first letter of this place
> Comes between *o* and *q*.
> Look under the cash register
> To find your next clue.

Oh boy! you think. *This is mysterious!*

You don't want to give up. If the clues lead to the Iceberg tipping photo, you'll be writing the biggest story in Club Penguin history!

You study the riddle. You can think of two places that begin with the letter *p* that have a cash register: the Pet Shop and the Pizza Parlor. Which one should you check out first?

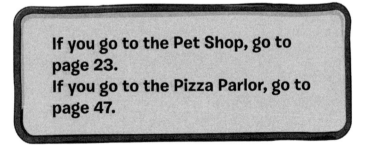

If you go to the Pet Shop, go to page 23.
If you go to the Pizza Parlor, go to page 47.

CONTINUED FROM PAGE 16.

"How about a sled race?" you say. "First to the bottom of the hill wins."

The Blue Team captain nods. "You're on! How about Penguin Run?"

It's a challenging run with a lot of obstacles to jump over. "Bring it on!" you say.

You all march over to the Ski Hill. The Red Team captain leads the other penguins to the bottom of Penguin Run to watch. You and the Blue Team captain take the ski lift to the top of the hill. You each grab a snow tube and ask a penguin nearby to count you off.

"On your mark, get set, go!"

You push off and start speeding down the hill. The first obstacle you come to is a low, snowy ridge. You soar over it and land perfectly without wiping out. You're doing great!

You maneuver around some logs and an icy pond. You jump over another ridge and you can see the finish line in sight. The Blue Team captain is close behind you.

Then, out of nowhere . . . *SLAM!* A penguin on a snow tube crashes into you. You fall out

71

of the tube and go tumbling into the snow. The penguin who crashed into you rushes up to you.

"Sorry," he says. "I was sledding down Express and I wiped out."

"It's okay," you say. Now you know how the Red Team captain feels! You were about to win that race.

You waddle down to the finish line. The Blue Team captain shakes your flipper.

"Good race," she says. "Too bad about that crash. We've got one contest left."

"How about a pizza-making contest?" someone in the crowd suggests.

You and the Blue Team captain both nod. There's only one thing to work out. There's a red lever on the Pizzatron 3000. Before you make pizzas, you can pull the lever to make candy pizzas or regular pizzas. What kind of pizzas should you make?

If you set the machine to make candy pizzas, go to page 45.
If you set the machine to make regular pizzas, go to page 17.

CONTINUED FROM PAGE 58.

You don't want to miss your deadline. You go back to the office and type your story.

A mysterious new group of penguins is causing a stir all over the island. Be on the lookout for the Surprise Snowball Society . . .

You write a few more paragraphs about the strange notes you received. Then you promise readers you will investigate to find out when the society will strike next. You print out the story and show it to Aunt Arctic.

"Very interesting," she says. "I'll put it in section B this week. You showed great determination following those notes. That's just the quality I need in my Lead Investigative Reporter. Would you like the position?"

You can't believe it. "Of course!" you say.

You grab your notebook and head back to the Town Center. You've got stories to investigate!

THE END

You head to the Coffee Shop and race upstairs to the Book Room. There are three lamps there, and you check them all, one by one. You find nothing. Just to be safe, you check every single book on the shelves. You look under every cushion.

Before you realize it, you've wasted nearly an hour looking for the clue. You're starting to get tired of following the clues anyway.

Discouraged, you go downstairs and sit at a table. A penguin wearing a green apron and glasses passes by and you flag him down.

"May I have a cup of hot chocolate, please?" you ask.

The penguin adjusts his eyeglasses. "I wish I could help, but I'm new at this. I can't seem to figure out how to pour beverages."

"Hey, it's easy," you say. "To pour drinks in the Coffee Shop, you need to wear the green apron, but you can't wear any other accessories. Just take off your glasses and you'll be fine."

The penguin takes off his glasses and pours you some hot chocolate.

"That's a great tip," he says. "You should print that in the newspaper."

Of course! Aunt Arctic loves to print tips in the newspaper. You gulp down your chocolate and head to the newspaper office. Aunt Arctic loves your tip.

"You have a flair for this," she says. "Can you write some more tips for the next issue?"

"Absolutely!" you say. You enjoy writing tips. It feels good to help other penguins. Though your search for the mysterious Iceberg tipping photo led you nowhere, you're happy that you've found something you're good at.

THE END

CONTINUED FROM PAGE 51.

You approach Hammer. "Excuse me," you say. "I'm from *The Club Penguin Times*. How did you feel when the light crashed?"

"I was scared!" Hammer says. "It just barely missed me. And we didn't get to finish the play."

"Why do you think it crashed?" you ask.

"The special effects director says it was a loose screw," Hammer says. "I hope it's fixed for the next performance. I just love being onstage! Hey, you should try it! The director's holding auditions later for the new play."

If you audition, you won't be able to finish your story. But being a star on stage sounds like just as much fun as being a star reporter—if not more. You decide to give it a try. First you call Aunt Arctic and tell her you're quitting the newspaper staff. She doesn't mind—she's got plenty of stories for the next issue.

"I'm going to audition," you tell Hammer. "Can you give me some tips?"

Hammer nods. "Sure thing."

THE END

CONTINUED FROM PAGE 57.

You decide to tackle the runs alphabetically. You grab a snow tube and slide down Penguin Run, avoiding obstacles on the way. You come to a smooth stop at the end of the run.

You start digging, right where you landed. The snow is deep. You dig until you hit something hard. You look down and see what looks like a piece of dark wood.

Excited, you dig around the wood. It's a treasure chest! You climb down into the hole you've dug and pry open the lid. You gasp.

The chest is filled with gold coins! You're stunned and confused. Did you find the treasure by accident, or was the mysterious penguin at the Iceberg behind it all somehow?

You lug the treasure chest onto your snow tube and drag it across the snow back to the newspaper office. Finding hidden treasure is a great story. And even if it doesn't make the front page, you're rich!

THE END

CONTINUED FROM PAGE 58.

You decide to take a risk and follow the footprints. They lead to the base of the mountains near the Dojo. As you get closer, you hear voices.

"I just know we'll be in *The Club Penguin Times* tomorrow," someone is saying.

"Soon everyone will know we are here!" says another penguin.

You slow down and hide behind a snowy rock. A small group of penguins wearing parkas and fuzzy boots are standing in a circle in the snow. You have found the Surprise Snowball Society! You step out into the open.

"Aha! I've found you!" you say.

The penguins turn to look at you.

"That's exactly what we wanted," says one.

You scratch your head. "I don't get it."

The penguins tell you that they used to meet every day at the Snow Forts for snowball fights. But then they decided they wanted to do something different from regular snowball fights.

"So we invented *surprise* snowball fights," one of the penguins explains. "We send messages to everyone in the group and tell them to meet at a certain place at a certain time. Then we surprise everyone there with a snowball fight!"

"That's why we called you," another penguin adds. "When the penguins read about this in the paper, we'll have lots more members."

You glance at your watch. "Yikes! If I don't hurry, there won't be a story in this week's paper. See you later!"

You hurry back to the newspaper office. Aunt Arctic rushes out of her office when she hears you come in.

"Is your story ready?" she asks.

"I didn't write the pizza story, I have another story for you," you promise.

You tell Aunt Arctic about the Surprise Snowball Society. She nods. "It's a good story, but I need it right away," she says.

"Give me three minutes," you say.

You type faster than you have ever typed before. You finish your story in record time. Aunt Arctic prints it, and the other reporters nickname you "Speedy." Cool!

THE END

The Blue Team captain looks like she might be tough to convince. You can tell she's very competitive.

Competitive. That gives you an idea. You gather up your courage and face her.

"I have a proposal for you," you tell her. "Let's have a competition. If I beat you, you'll do the rematch. If I lose, the Blue Team walks away with the win."

She doesn't even have to think about it. "It's a deal!" she says. Her eyes are shining with excitement. "What kind of contest are we talking about here?"

You hadn't thought your plan through that far. You should probably pick something you're good at.

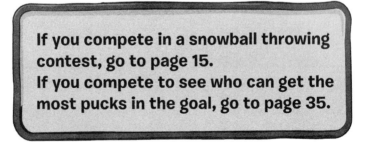

If you compete in a snowball throwing contest, go to page 15.
If you compete to see who can get the most pucks in the goal, go to page 35.